OWEN'S HEART:

A BWWM SMALL TOWN ROMANCE

THERESA HODGE

SHANI GREENE-DOWDELL

TABLE OF CONTENTS

This book is dedicated to anyone who
believes in second chances.

CHAPTER
one

OWEN

I can smell the sweet-spicy scent of cinnamon as I walk into Mildred's Cafe. "Good morning, Mr. Clemonte," Mildred calls out as I enter the building.

Mildred Brown is the owner of the café and has a hands-on approach to her business. She is a feisty sixty-something-year-old woman with smooth, ebony skin that contradicts her years.

"Good morning," I reply, stepping up to the counter. "Now, Mildred, what have I told you about calling me Mr. Clemonte? I'm just plain old Owen."

"There is nothing plain about you, Owen," Mildred lets loose a chuckle. "You and your brothers are every bit as handsome as your dad. May the good Lord rest his soul. That was a good man, and he raised yawl boys rightly into great men," Mildred went on to say.

"I thank you kindly," I reply, giving her a wink before taking a seat on one of the stools.

"Where are your brothers, by the way. You three usually come in for breakfast together on a Saturday."

My brothers Lance, Anson, and I are the owners of Clemonte Ranch in Prattville, Alabama. I'm the youngest at thirty-one, Lance is thirty-three, and Anson the oldest is thirty-five. Our father Hank left us equal shares in the business after he died a year ago from a heart attack at sixty-five. Our mother, Virginia, had died five years earlier from liver cancer.

We missed our parents something fierce even if we were all able-bodied grown men. The ranch was flourishing thanks to our combined efforts. Lance is the accountant and makes sure everything is in order with our finances. He has always been a wiz with numbers. Anson and I handle mostly everything else, along with the additional employees we hire around the ranch.

"Anson is on a business trip. He had a lead on some cattle out in Texas. Lance is busy this morning so that just leaves me."

Mildred gives me a sweet smile. "Well, what will you have this morning, Owen?"

"Give me the usual. Pancakes, bacon, sunny side up eggs, and a cup of black coffee."

"Got it," Mildred replies. I'll have the waitress bring it right out," she adds before going through a set of swinging doors that lead to the kitchen.

I glance around the café. It's not too busy this early, but I know the crowd will pick up as the day goes on. Ten minutes later, a plate filled with my favorite meal is placed before me.

"Here you go," a familiar voice that I know all too well

says.

My head jerks around. My eyes clash with a pair of dark brown eyes. My heart slams against my chest. "When did you come back here," the words slip past my lips in shock.

"Here's your coffee," Rania Brown, a girl I dated through college, says dryly. She's not just any girl, but the love of my life. She sits my mug beside my plate with a light thud. "Will there be anything else, Mr. Clemonte?"

With my question ignored, it only makes me have more.

"Rania?" I will my heart rate to slow down as I take her in. I haven't seen Rania since I graduated from the University of Alabama. Rania had been a Junior back then. She had broken up with me over something ridiculous.

I can't help but take in her shoulder-length black hair pulled back into a low ponytail. I take in her dark, relax-fitted blue jeans and a plain black buttoned-down collared shirt with the lettering Mildred's Café engraved into the upper right side.

Rania is more beautiful than the last time I saw her almost ten years ago.

A region of my lower half starts to react from the familiar smell permeating my nostrils. The scent is all Rania. I missed it. I didn't know how much until I was in her presence again.

"Are you back home for good? Are you working for your aunt now?" I question her, my food forgotten.

"If you must know, my Aunt is having knee surgery soon. Since I'm the only family she got that she can count on, I'm here to run the café until she can take over again. Does that answer your question?"

All the old feelings I felt for Rania start to resurface again. My love for Rania is a living and moving thing that has a heart of its own. I can't stop having feelings for her.

When she was staying in New York, I could pretend that the feelings I had for Rania didn't exist. But with her standing here in front of me, I can't deny the love I had for her in the past is still as real today as it was then.

My stare continues to stray over her curves. Rania Brown is all woman, and the dark honey of her skin has a healthy, supple glow to it. The college Rania has nothing on the beautiful woman standing before me. Her full hips have rounded even more, and her full C cup breasts make me want to reach out and test their softness in my hands.

"My eyes are up here, cowboy," Rania's voice cuts into my perusal.

My green eyes slowly travel back up to hers, and a slow grin arches one side of my mouth. Rania is absolutely gorgeous, and I have to make her mine again.

"Indeed they are, and what beautiful eyes they are too." I stare at her long enough to capture a picture of her orbs that are beautiful enough to write a song about into my mind.

Rania lets out a breath of frustration, and her eyes roll up toward the ceiling before meeting mine again.

"Well, it's been grand catching up again, but as you can see, I have work to do," she says, motioning to other customers that had arrived since I came in.

"I understand sweetheart. Don't let me stop you." I tilt my cowboy hat and give her a wink. "Since I know you're going to be around a while, I plan on seeing a lot of you."

"Seeing is all you will be doing, Owen, since I don't suppose I can stop you from that."

I chuckle. "Is that a dare, darlin'?"

"No, that's a fact," she snipes. "Enjoy your breakfast. If

there is anything else you need, Sandra will help you." She points to the other waitress that walks up to the counter.

I briefly glance at Sandra before glancing back at Rania. "I won't need anything else for now. You have everything I need," I tell her before she walks off in a huff.

I look up just in time to see Mildred peeping her graying head of hair around the swinging doors. She gives me a mischievous smile and wink before slipping back into the kitchen.

Well, I be damned. I do believe Mildred is playing matchmaker. I grin and dig into my breakfast with relish. Rania may try to run from me, but it won't be long before I have her with me and beneath me where she belongs.

CHAPTER

two

RANIA

"What was that about, auntie?" I gripe when I enter the kitchen after serving Owen his breakfast.

"What was what about?" Aunt Mildred looks at me with a coy grin. "We have tables that need to be served, and you're the server, so I sent you to serve Owen his food."

"Right, but Owen? You know how I feel about him, and you pulled me off of food prep and made me a server today, just in time for me to serve him his breakfast."

Aunt Mildred gasps in mock surprise. Touching her imaginary pearls, she asserts, "Why I would never."

Oh, yes, she would.

I harrumph my disapproval. "Well, I told him Sandra will be serving him because I'll be staying back here until he leaves. I don't want to deal with him out of the blue like this," I fuss.

"Fine then." My aunt shrugs and looks at me like I don't know my head from my tail. "Stay back here and hide from the man if that's what you prefer," she says with a hint of

10

sarcasm.

I feel like she has more to say to me, like her last words imply that I'm hiding like a chicken. That's not the case. If a person puts something behind them, it's not wise to keep interacting with it. I'm simply trying to leave Owen where he belongs, in the past. A beautiful past. So beautiful.

Well, that was the way it was until the moment it became so ugly.

I try to stop thinking about him over the next hour. I remain in the kitchen, chopping onions and peppers and slicing lemons and oranges, along with any other thing that needs to be done.

I lose the battle with my mind over leaving Owen in the past. All I can think about is the time when me and Owen were in love.

The next thing I know, I'm drifting back to freshman year in 2010. My best friend, Janae, had her doubts about us, but I was so sure of our relationship that I had no problem expressing my certainty to her.

"I can't believe you haven't had sex with Owen Clemonte yet. I don't know how you stand to be around him and not go there. Oh, Lord!" Janae says, using her hand to fan her cheeks. "Aren't you afraid that he will sleep with one of the many girls that are always vying for his attention?"

"Owen isn't like that. Even though we've been dating for almost a year, he doesn't want to rush me. He says he will wait until I'm ready."

"Do you believe him?" Janae asks as she flops down on top of my bed.

"Of course I do. Owen has never given me a reason to think otherwise. I trust him. I think I've finally found my person in Owen." I smile, thinking about the way he treats me. He goes out of his way to

make me feel like I'm the luckiest girl in the world, though we have yet to have our first sexual experience.

"That's great, but you are better than me," Janae continues while I fold up my clean laundry and put it away.

"I love Owen, and he loves me. There is more to our relationship than sex, Janae. How many boyfriends have you went through this year alone?" I ask though I know the answer to that. My friend has been busy during our freshman year in college.

Janae's mouth opens and closes. Her light brown eyes narrow into a piercing stare.

"Are you calling me a slut, Rania?"

"No! I spit out. I was just saying..."

"I'm just messing with you. I know I go through boyfriends fast, but I swear I don't give up the goodies to all of them. I know what the guys say about me, but the truth is that I love sex. If guys can take what they want and drop a girl after getting it, then so can I. I refuse to feel bad about what I like."

"I wish I could be more like you. I love how outspoken you are, and you never give a damn about how anyone thinks," I tell her.

"Trust me when I say this, worrying about what others think is a waste of your energy," Janae advises. "I learned a long time ago that being a people pleaser will lead to depression. My own mother taught me that, Rania."

Janae reaches for a clean towel and starts to fold it. She helps me make quick work of putting away my clean laundry while a heavy silence hangs over us.

I remember Janae said her mother took kindness to an all-new level. So much so that she became a doormat for family and friends. Eventually, they took so much out of her that she started drinking to cope with mundane stuff day in and day out. It was a vicious cycle that consumed her mother. Janae has been determined not to let that happen to her.

"I'm hungry," Janae suddenly says. "Let's go out for pizza. My treat!"

"Since you mentioned it, I'm hungry too. I'll treat us next time."

Even though I know I should be spending my time studying, I can't help but jump at the chance of going to the on-campus pizza shop.

That's another thing about Janae. She is outgoing and has loads of friends she hangs out with all the time. She attempts to get me to go out with them. Sometimes I do, but most times, I hole up in my dorm room studying. The rest of my free time is designated for spending with Owen when he doesn't have his sports or fraternity meetings and working a few hours at the bookstore three days a week.

"What the hell?" Janae says, stepping into the pizza shop. She nudges me with her shoulder and points.

I glance up to see Chantel Washington all up in Owen's face. What the hell is right? My blood begins to boil because of Chantel, the president of one of the most supercilious sororities on campus, which happens to be the sisters to Owen's fraternity. I don't use the word hate often, but I hate Chantel with a passion. She has her sights on Owen, whether he's my boyfriend or not.

"Do you want me to grab her by her blond curls and snatch her away from your boyfriend? You know a Sistah got your back," Janae says as she glares at Owen and Chantel, who is sitting at the table with some more of her sorority sisters and Owen's frat brothers.

"No. Let's just grab a table and ignore them," I reply, not wanting to make a scene. Plus, I didn't want to appear jealous every time I saw Owen talking to another girl. I never wanted to be that kind of insecure person. Even if I was boiling with jealousy on the inside at this moment.

In truth, what woman wouldn't want Owen Clemonte? By far, he is the hottest and most liked guy on campus and, in my book, the most alluring. My body heats up every time I'm around him. I don't know how I've held off giving my virginity to him this long because he makes me wet every time he gives me that charming smile of his. Every time I look into his sexy green eyes, I lose a bit of my control.

"Hey, Rania!" Owen's friend Brad calls out to me just as Janae and I are grabbing a table.

When I glance over my shoulder, Owen and my gazes clash. His eyes light up. He jumps up from the table with his friends and strolls over in my direction. I give Brad a limp wave and attach a nonchalant smile to my full lips.

"Hey babe, I thought you were gonna stay in and study," Owen says as he leans in to give me a soft kiss on my lips.

"I bet you did," Janae replies before I can say anything. "I guess boys will be boys when their girlfriend isn't around, huh?"

"What's that supposed to mean?" Owen's gaze slides over to my friend, giving her a narrowed-eye look.

"You know damn well what that means, Owen. You let that slut hang all over you like you don't have a girlfriend. The disrespect is real, I tell you," she huffs.

I suddenly decide I don't even want to dine in. I rather take the pizza back to the dorm instead. "Janae, can you go ahead and order our pizza to go? I'll catch up with you in a few," I tell her pushing her towards the counter.

Janae glares at Owen before turning to me as she walks away. She gives me a knowing smile as she walks toward the counter.

"What got your girl's panties in a twist?" Owen asks, settling his hands on my shoulder.

I shrug his hands off me instead of answering his question. "Go back and hang out with your friends, Owen. Janae and I just came in to grab a pizza, and then I'm going back to the dorm to study."

"Why don't you and Janae come and hang out with us?"

I glance over Owen's shoulder to be met with the glaring blue gaze of Chantel's and the rest of her minions.

"No, I need to get back and finish my essay along with more studying. I have a scholarship to upkeep. I can't let my average drop, or I will lose it. You know that my parents don't have the money to pay for me to be here."

"I have money, Rania. You already know that anything you need and it's yours."

"That's your inheritance from your grandparents, Owen. I'm not some charity case. I have money from working at the bookstore part-time three days a week."

"I know how independent you are, sweetheart, but I'm your man, and I want to take care of you," he says, leaning down to peer into my eyes. Amidst the college crowd, I get lost in his earnest gaze. Owen's woodsy scent with an undertone of citrus cologne wafts through my nostrils.

My tongue swipes against my bottom lip, and Owen's gaze follows the movement of my tongue. My nipples stand to attention under my University of Alabama tee shirt and press against the lacy material of my white bra.

"Don't do that," Owen's voice becomes a low growl against my ear.

"Do what?" I gaze up at him, and my breath catches in my throat when he presses closer against me. I attempt to take a step back, but he follows me.

"You know what it does to me whenever you lick your lips, sweetheart. I want to—"

My hands grip Owen's tank top. I don't know what's getting into me, but I want him to take me back to his dorm and make love to me right this instant. My will power about not having sex just went out the window.

Owen is still giving me that penetrating stare. My stomach muscle clenches, so does the core of my pussy. "Let's get outta here. We can go back—" Owen starts when Janae walks up.

"I got the pizza! Are you ready to jet?" she asks, officially cutting off whatever Owen was going to say.

I breathe a sigh of relief and release my grip from clenching Owen's tank top.

"Yeah, I'm ready." I back away from Owen, and I'm just about to turn away when he grabs my wrist and pulls me back to him.

"Are you leaving without giving your man a goodbye kiss? I don't think so," he answers his own question and pulls me into his arms.

Owen's lips slam down on mine. My mouth automatically opens to receive his thrusting tongue. His kiss is deep and seductive as his tongue slides against my own. A soft moan slips past my lips, but Owen swallows it.

"You do know that you are the only woman for me, right?" He mutters against my mouth.

I can only moan my agreement as the kiss deepens even further.

"Ahem," the clearing of Janae's throat penetrates through my foggy brain. Then chants of Owen's frat brother's across the room have me pulling away from him.

"Get a room, you two," his friend Brad calls out.

Owen shakes his head as if to clear it. One side of his mouth tilts into a sexy grin. "That's not a bad idea," Owen says, searing me with his hot gaze.

"No way!" Janae pulls me away and out the door before I can make up my mind to stay or go.

"I'll call you later," Owen calls out as I glance over my shoulder.

I smile and nod. At that moment, I know that there was no way I would give my boyfriend up to the likes of Chantel. It doesn't matter how many tricks she pulls by trying to get with him. Owen is mine, and I am his, and nothing else matters in the scheme of things.

"Don't you think we have enough sliced lemons?" Aunt Mildred's question pulls me out of my trip down memory lane.

Coming out of my reverie, I glance down at the table. I have cut every lemon in the refrigerator and put them in five large containers. "Too many, huh?" I ask.

She shakes her head in disbelief. "Young lady, one day you'll realize what your problem is." She nods toward the bustling dining area. "And it just walked out the door."

"Who, Owen?"

"Don't turn into an owl on me. Yes, your guy is gone."

"He's not mine," I protest.

A harumphing sound is my aunt's reply.

I shrug. "I have more prep to do, so I should get back to it."

"Whatever you do, please don't slice up any more fruit or vegetables. I think we have enough to last for the entire week. It would be better for you to go out with Owen than to make all of my perishables go bad too soon."

"I won't cut anything else today." I chuckle and walk out of the kitchen to stock the worker stations. There will be no date with Owen. I know that, but I have to keep reminding my aunt that he's not mine.

Once upon a time, I never would have been able to say

that Owen wasn't mine, but now it's a harsh reality that I have come to grips with. No matter what my aunt is up to, I can't allow coming back to Prattville to drag those old feelings out of me. I can't.

CHAPTER *three*

OWEN

The next morning, I gulp down a cup of black coffee as I stand on the balcony taking in the clear blue sky and inhaling the smell of the ranch. Curing hay, mixed with the rich turned soil, and the manure from the cattle and horses and the longleaf pine's scent in plentiful supply, permeate my nostrils. This is undoubtedly heaven on God's green earth. There is only one thing missing.

The image of Rania enters my mind. She is more beautiful than she was years ago, and that's saying a lot since she is the most beautiful woman that I've ever had the pleasure of loving. I wanted to feast on her presence yesterday when I saw her, but I could tell Rania wanted nothing to do with me. Rania is just as feisty as ever, but I promise myself I won't let her run away from me like she did all those years ago because of a blatant misunderstanding and a bald-faced lie.

Damn Chantel and her conniving ways. Her lie caused me

the only woman I ever loved. The only woman I could ever love. Other women have paled in comparison to Rania over the years.

"Hey, little bro." Lance walks out onto the balcony with a cup of coffee in hand. "You look like you're in deep thought there. What's up?"

"Rania is back in town. I saw her yesterday at her aunt's café. She's working there now to help Mildred out."

"Whew!" My brother lets loose a long breath as he walks up to the railing and leans his hip against it. "How did you feel about seeing her after so long a time?"

"I'm not gonna lie, bro. It felt damn good. My heart threatened to slam out of my chest at the sight of her. When I talked to Mildred, she didn't even let on that Rania was back in town. I wanted to grab her and bring her back to the ranch. I wanted to haul her up to my bedroom and never let her go."

My brother chuckles. "Hold your horse's bro. If I know anything about women and you do too, it's not going to be that easy to get Rania into your bed. Patience wins the race, bro."

"Yeah, I know, but I used all my patience years ago getting her into my bed. I had her in my arms one damn time, Lance, and then all of it went up in smoke. All because Rania didn't trust my love for her. How could she think I would ever make love to someone else. She was it for me."

"Owen, you two were young back then, and Rania was even younger. What was she when you two broke up, nineteen or twenty? Girls that age don't have their emotions under control and usually make rash decisions."

I shrug my shoulder at the thought of Rania back then.

"Rania wasn't like other girls her age when we were in university. She was smart, independent, and mature. When the rest of us wanted to party, Rania was busy with her head in a book or working at the bookstore. I admired how focused she was. When she broke up with me right before my graduation, I was shocked to learn how insecure she had been in our relationship."

"But didn't you tell me how Chantel was always flirting with you? Plus the countless of other girls around campus? Sooner or later, you had to know that would get to any woman. Did you at least set boundaries when it came to Chantel?" my brother asked.

"Chantel or any other girl didn't mean anything to me. I only saw Rania, and it didn't matter what any other of them tried; my loyalty was to Rania. Man, she broke my fucking heart when she left me!"

"Alright, I get what you're saying, Owen. Calm down. I'm on your side. I'll always be on your side."

I nod at Lance and take in a deep calming breath, but my mind can't help but go back to the day Rania made my life explode to shit.

"Hey babe, I have less than two hours before graduation. I'm coming by early to pick you up because I want my girl front and center," I say to Rania over my cell phone.

"I'm not coming to your graduation. Owen, how could you do something like that to me?"

I frown, tilting my head to the side as worry lines furrow the space between my brows. *"What are you talking about? What's wrong, sweetheart?"*

"Don't you sweetheart me! Don't ever call me sweetheart again. You

got that Owen Levi Clemonte!"

"Hey, calm down. I'm coming—"

"I know you had Chantel in your dorm room last night. I saw the two of you making out. Her friend Jasmine sent me the pictures. How the hell could you do that to us, Owen? Chantel of all the girls on campus. You knew how much I detested her. I will never forgive you for this. Do you hear me?" Rania shouts so loud I have to pull the phone away from my ear.

Fuck! I didn't even know that someone took a picture of Chantel when she caught me off guard and kissed me. It's true that I shouldn't have had her in my dorm room in the first place, but it was nothing more than us sitting around drinking and having a good time before graduation. I had invited Rania to hang with us, but she wanted to cram for an accounting exam coming up in less than a week. I understood and didn't push her to come... Now I wished I did.

"Rania, I'm coming over to explain. I promise you it's not what it looks like. I swear to you."

"Go to hell, Owen. I don't believe anything you say. I won't trust anything you say again!"

"Fuck! Listen to me." I rush out of my dorm, all the while trying to convince her that nothing happened. "Baby, I'll explain everything to you when I arrive at your dorm. I need to talk to you face to face. Okay, sweetheart?"

"I said, don't call me that. Besides, I'm not in my dorm room because I knew you would rush over here to try to get out of your lies. I always knew you wanted that girl. Why else would you allow her to hang all over you? I hate you, Owen, and I hate Chantel even more!"

"Baby, please don't do this to us." I run across campus, trying to get to Rania as fast as I can. We aren't going out like this. I am not about to

lose the best thing that ever happened to me over such a misunderstanding. I swear, as God is my witness, I would never cheat on Rania. I can't even get hard for any girl besides her. She just has to believe me.

"Let me in, Rania!" My fist raps incessantly against the wooden door. I knock so hard I can feel the door rattle against its frame.

The door swings open.

"What the hell do you want, Owen?"

"Where is Rania?" I brush past Rania's friend and roommate, Janae.

"She isn't here."

"Then, where the hell is she?" I whip around to glare at her.

A smirky smile appears on her lips. "Do you think I would tell you after the way you hurt her? I told her not to trust you as much as she did. I warned her boys would be boys, and you surely proved my point."

"You need to stay out of this and mind your own fucking business! I knew you always had it in for me. You never wanted Rania and me together anyway," I growl out angrily.

"That's where you're wrong, Owen. I hoped to be wrong, but Rania saw the way Chantel hangs all over you the same way that I did. You didn't respect Rania to set boundaries with all of these other tramps on campus. How would you feel seeing other guys all up on Rania, huh?"

"I would kill every fucking one of them," I spit out. "Janae, I beg you. Please tell me where I can find Rania. I swear to you, that picture was misleading. I need to explain that to my girl."

"I can't tell you where she is, Owen. I promised her, and I'm going to keep my word."

"I'm not going to listen to this shit," I tell her and storm towards Rania's closed bedroom door, but she's not there when I enter the room.

"Don't you have an Honor speech to give or something?"

"Fuck graduation and fuck you too for standing between us!" I storm out the room and through the women's dorm. I question everyone I make contact with, asking if they've seen Rania. No one has.

I don't find Rania that day or the day after. I learn later that she took her exam early and left campus for the summer. By the time I make it home back to Prattville, I'm a mess.

A fucked up mess.

"Hey Owen, did you hear me?"

"No, I'm sorry. My head was somewhere else."

"I said, Joe and Rick are coming by to mend the fences that the cattle broke through last night. Let's go give them a hand. It will help get your mind off of things for a while," Lance suggests.

"You're right. I need to pull my head outta my ass and get to work. Let's go, I tell him heading into the house to put my coffee cup in the sink and then out the door. I have a gut feeling there is only a matter of time before I have my woman back in my arms where she belongs.

CHAPTER
four

RANIA

Monday...
Two Days Later

Damn it! Ever since I saw Owen, I haven't been able to get him off of my mind. The sight of him made me want to fall back into his arms again. I knew deep down I never got over him, and I never would. The few relationships I had since Owen attest to that very fact.

Sometimes, I wonder if I would have gone back to Owen had he found me after I had broken up with him? Thanks to Janae, I'd hidden out with other friends around campus until I took my exam, then I went home with her for the summer. I had made Aunt Mildred promise not to tell Owen where I had gone, and she kept her word even though she hated the fact that Owen and I were broken up.

Janae was glad to have me with her for the summer until we both went back to campus in the fall. Her mother was a complete mess back then, drinking herself into oblivion. Thank God that Helen has found the help she needed since then and has been five years on the road to sobriety.

Janae and I even got jobs at the local Dairy Queen in Gadsden, Alabama, where she lived. I miss Janae so much. I'm happy that she's now married with two kids of her own. She's a mom, which I thought would never be. She promised that she never wanted to settle down, least of all have children. I guess meeting a good man like Jonah will do that to a woman.

I'm happy for Janae, and we speak and facetime often. Since I live so far away in New York, working and living in the Bay Ridge area, I haven't seen Janae since we graduated from university eight years ago. Janae went back home to Gadsden and got a job with a local law office, the same office where she met Jonah, who she later fell in love with and married. On the other hand, I was blessed to get an internship with Cohen & Resnick, an accounting firm.

I thanked God back then that Bay Ridge was a residential area about twice the size of Prattville. It wasn't too hard for me to get a feel for the city, even though it was on a faster scale and far more citified than Prattville, Alabama. After about a year, I was offered a full-time position. I hardly made it back home to visit Aunt Mildred, but when she called me a few weeks ago telling me of her surgery, I put in for an extended leave and came to help her with the café.

Aunt Mildred is my dad's sister and had never married. We have relatives dotted over the state of Alabama here and there, but none are close and dependable. My aunt took me in at a time when I needed her the most, and there is no way I would let her down.

Parking at the café, I head inside the building to start my day. I turn on the lights and head over to the back office to put my handbag away. The rest of the employees soon arrive, and the business is bustling with the smells of coffee, bacon, and all the good things morning in the café brings.

I talked my aunt into staying home to rest up for her upcoming surgery. She will be checking in at Elmore Regional on Wednesday morning to prepare for surgery in the afternoon.

My expertise is accounting, but I've been working in the café with my aunt most summers since I was sixteen. The café s pretty busy during the morning hours, but the crowd thins out an hour before the lunch hour begins. I'm already tired since I didn't get much sleep last night nor the night before. Images of Owen kept digging into my thoughts and dreams.

Last night, my dreams were filled with making love to Owen. I swear I could smell the scent of his woodsy, citrusy cologne, and I could hear the deep grate of his voice as he plunged deep inside my silken heat. I woke up burning for Owen's touch and saturated in wetness between my thighs. How the hell am I going to bear being around him if my body becomes aflame with a desire so severe that it causes my panties to become wet every time I see him?

Right now, my nipples harden at the thought of Owen kissing me again. I remember how Owen used to murmur against my ear when we were in a crowd how much he loved me and how much he wanted me. He even promised that he would never allow anything to tear us apart and that we would be together forever.

That had been proven to be nothing but lies.

Even though in the beginning, Owen called me, emailed, and texted me incessantly... soon the calls and text messages became fewer. By the time summer was over and fall began, hearing from him had become nonexistent. I knew that he had quickly moved on with his life from things my aunt implied but wouldn't come straight out and say.

On many occasions, I had wished that I had stayed in contact with a few of my high school friends back home to keep in the loop about Owen since he didn't do the social media scene at all.

I grab a cup of coffee, add sugar and a splash of milk before taking a seat on a barstool. Maybe the caffeine will give me energy since I still have a long day ahead of me. My aunt hired someone to take over in case I need to be away, so I won't run myself ragged, but I need to stay busy to keep my mind off of someone I rather not think about. I have given them too much power over my brain as is.

"Oh, my God! Rania Brown! Is that really you?" A voice I remember well causes me to spin around on the barstool and face the entrance of the café.

I sit my coffee cup down, and a smile plasters against my lips. "Desiree Ellis!" I exclaim and hop up from the barstool.

She's smiling so hard as we meet each other halfway and go in for a hug.

"How many years has it been, girl?" she asks.

"I don't know, maybe close to six years."

"It's something like that or nearly. Last time I heard you were living in New York. Are you back home now?"

"Yes, I am. My aunt is having surgery, so I came home to help her out. "I missed you so much, Desiree. I'm sorry we lost touch when I went away to college."

"Don't sweat it, Rania. That works both ways, doesn't it?"

I nod, but still, the smile on my lips won't let up. Desiree still looks the same, only her hair is cut into a short bob. It fits her round face; her dark brown skin is radiant without one blemish.

She's plumper than she was years ago, but the extra weight really looks good on her. Her dark brown eyes are still looking me over the same way I'm taking my old best friend from my high school days in.

"You know when we went to rival universities, I to Auburn and you to the University of Alabama, we were bound to lose touch. Being on campus at Auburn was a whole different experience from high school."

"Tell me about it," I agree. University life was a different kind of life altogether. "So what can I get you?"

"Can I get two chicken tender plates with all the trimmings to go? I have to get back to work at the courthouse. I work in the paralegal department," she states.

"That's great, Desiree! Let me give your order to the cook. It won't take long."

"Great." She nods and takes a seat at the counter while I go back to personally give the cook my friend's order.

While Desiree waits, I sit with her since the other waitresses can handle the few customers dotted around the building.

"Are you married or have kids?" Desiree asks as we catch up on old times.

I shake my head. "No."

"Boyfriend?"

I manage to keep a pleasant look on my face when I answer, "Nope, there is no one special at the moment. My job has been my whole livelihood. What about you?"

"I'm engaged," Desiree says with a huge smile. "Do you remember Thomas Ray? He graduated the same year Owen Clemonte did. She extends her hand, and I take in her square-cut diamond. I didn't know much about diamonds, but the sparkle is brilliant, and it looks flawlessly cut.

A tremble travels up my spine at the mention of Owen. But I ooh and ahh over the ring to dismiss my discomfort.

"Yes, I remember Thomas. His family owns the hardware store, right?"

"Right! Now Thomas runs the business since his dad retired. Regina, his sister, didn't want anything to do with it. She got married years ago and moved to Colorado."

"Wow, I'm happy for you. Congratulations!"

"Thank you, Rania. Speaking of Owen, I remember you having a crush on him in high school. I heard from your aunt that you two started dating in college, but when I graduated and moved back home, I heard the two of you had broken up. What happened with you two? I always thought you would make the perfect couple."

"Two chicken tender specials are up," the cook taps a bell as he calls out.

"Well, your order is up, and it's on the house," I tell her when she starts to take out her wallet. "We will catch up another time, and I will tell you all about it, okay?"

"Sure thing, and thank you for lunch. Give me your number, and we will get together soon," Desiree takes out her cell and hands it over to me. I add my number to her contact list and call my cell. I hang up before it goes to voicemail, so she has my cell number too.

"It's really great to see you again, Rania. Having you back

home will be like old times."

"Yeah, it will," I reply.

We hug again before she leaves. I walk her to the door and turn around to head back to the counter. But the door opens again. I turn around to greet the customer when my eyes land on the last person I need to see.

Owen.

CHAPTER

five

OWEN

Rania's brown gaze clashes with mine. A sight so beautiful that I know there is a God sitting high, who has mercy on my soul.

"Rania," I call out to her, unable to not call her name upon laying eyes on her.

"What do you want, Owen?" she asks but stands rooted to her spot as I walk closer to her.

"Can we talk?"

Rania glances around the café, which isn't super busy at the moment. "The late lunch crowd will be arriving soon, and I will be busy."

"Yeah. I know. I—can we have dinner later?"

Rania's brown eyes slowly rake over me, from my red and black checkered long sleeve shirt to my well-fitting wrangler jeans. Her eyes pause midpoint near my leather belt before moving on down to my scuffed brown oiled leather boots.

I use the time to take her in as well. She's sexy as fuck, so hell yeah, I'm absorbing every detail about her into my mind. Rania is still gorgeous in her work uniform. Her mid-length hair is held in a loose ponytail at the top of her head. My heart begins to patter against my chest in hopes that she will say yes to having dinner with me.

"Owen, I'm going to be busy at the café, and in between that time, I will be taking care of my Aunt Mildred after her knee surgery."

"Your aunt told me that after she gets from the hospital that her doctor arranged for her to have in-home care, but she preferred to go to the local inpatient rehabilitation facility. She said she wants to use her six weeks of recovering like a mini-vacation she never had."

Rania's mouth drops open as if she is surprised that I know of her aunt's plans.

She clears her throat before meeting my green eyes. "Well, clearly, you've been talking to my aunt behind my back because she never mentioned that you've talked. I'm still busy," she adds.

My lips automatically turn up at the corners, and amusement enters my eyes.

"Your aunt also told me she hired someone to help you out around here. She said she couldn't have her only niece working herself to the bone."

More merriment enters my eyes when Rania glances away from me. She seems to be momentarily at a loss for words. Finally, she turns her beautiful eyes on me and graces me with a long glance.

"When did you want to go out to dinner? It can't be tomorrow because my aunt is having surgery early Wednesday morning, and we'll be getting ready for it tomorrow night."

"I know. We can have dinner on Friday night or Saturday if you prefer. Or we could do both," I say, giving her a confident smile.

"You're so full of knowledge today, aren't you, Owen? If you must know, I already have plans for this weekend."

"With who?" The smile that is attached to my lips suddenly slides away.

RANIA

"**I guess my aunt doesn't tell you everything,**" I taunt Owen.

I feel great pleasure in knocking that cocky assed smile off his face. How dare he show up looking all handsome in his tight jeans looking all sexy, smelling good enough to devour, and as confident as always.

I've matured a lot since I was in university. I've lived life on my own while working and navigating a new city. I may have been a country naïve girl when I left Alabama, but I've returned full grown and full of enlightenment for men like

Owen. I'm sure the rumors I heard of his womanizing ways were true. He may have fooled me once but never twice.

"I want to know who you have plans with this weekend, Rania."

"Owen, lower your voice!" I pull him aside as a couple enters the restaurant. I greet them and give the couple a warm smile before pulling Owen back into the small office that I'm now using that belongs to my aunt.

I open the door, step inside, and Owen walks in behind me. He kicks the door close with the heel of his boot, faces me, and crosses his arms across his muscular chest.

"Let's get this straight," I start talking as soon as we are alone. "I don't owe you an explanation about who I go out with. The last time I checked, I was a grown woman of twenty-nine. What gives you the right anyway?"

"Fuck!" Owen tugs on the thick strands of his wavy hair. "You're right. You don't owe me an explanation, but I would prefer one nonetheless."

"Do I ask about who you're dating? From what I heard since being back, you keep your dating card pretty full."

"Those women don't mean shit compared to you, Rania. Consider them gone. Give me another chance, and I promise there will be only you."

"Yeah, I've heard that promise before."

"Stop. Please give us one chance to talk. I won't push. After one dinner, if you never want to see me again, I will honor your decision."

I let out a long breath. "Okay, one dinner Owen. We can meet up on Saturday night. Where do you want to meet?"

"No, I will pick you up at seven at your aunt's place." Owen gives me an enigmatic smile. My stomach flip-flops from the happiness in his green eyes.

"Okay, but remember it's just to talk and nothing else."

"Of course," he agrees and pulls me into a tight embrace before I can stop him.

I shrug from his embrace before I have the chance to relish in his smell and strength. "Go," I say, stepping away from him to open the office door. "I need to get back to work."

"Sure thing, sweetheart." Owen gives me a wink before sauntering out the door.

I follow him at a slower pace and watch him exit the café.

Damn it, why didn't I remain adamant and just say no to Owen?

You know why, my inner voice scolds me. *It's because you never stopped loving the man... not even once.*

I keep as busy as I can for the rest of the day in hopes of keeping thoughts of Owen at bay.

OWEN

Saturday Night

I blow out a long breath as I drive up to Mildred's white clapboard home with black shudders. It feels like I'm back in school and about to hang out with Rania. The old house still looks as inviting as it did years ago when I was eager to spend time with the smartest girl at school.

I walk up the paved sidewalk toward the porch. Rania meets me at the door wearing a beautiful blue jean dress and black heels. I smile, knowing that she would look stunning in anything. Tonight is no different.

"Hey, I saw you pull up," she says and offers me a smile along with her greeting. "Give me just a second to grab my purse, and I'll be ready to go."

"I'll be right here," I tell her and glance around the tidy living room, hoping to spot Mildred.

Rania comes back to the door with her purse in hand. "Are you looking for something?"

"Is Mildred home?" I ask, checking on my one and only true ally in my long-shot quest to get Rania back.

"No, she's not here. She's staying in the rehabilitation center to help her recover from surgery, remember?"

"Oh, that's right." I snap my fingers. "I hope she gets well soon because I can't wait until my friend gets home. I've been thinking about her." Having Mildred around lifts everyone's spirits in the town, especially those who come through her cafe's doors. So, I do want her to have a speedy recovery.

"That makes two of us. I miss her too," Rania acknowledges.

I motion for Rania to walk ahead of me to the car, unknowingly torturing myself with the sight displayed before me now. It's enough to make a grown man cry. Her voluptuous hips sashaying from side to side drag up the lust I thought I successfully pushed down. But hell no, until I can claim the lovely black queen walking toward my car, I'm still just as fucked as I was before she accepted my offer for a date.

"You look beautiful," I tell her as I open the door to let her in.

"Thanks. You're not too bad yourself," she replies with a coy grin.

With Rania secure inside my Jeep, I rush around and slide into the driver's seat.

As soon as the engine roars to life, she asks, "Where are

we going?"

"Well, I was thinking that it's been a while since we've been to KimberLia's," I begin.

"KimberLia's, wow! You're right. It's been forever since we have gone there."

"It's been a long time since we have done anything, Rania." Thoughts of the one time we made love cause my rogue lower region to twitch with an understanding of this statement.

"True," is her one-word answer. Rania takes her attention back from me and starts staring at the passing roadside scenery.

Craving to have her brown eyes trained on me again, I remind her, "We have some great memories at KimberLia's. Great times."

"I know," she says and steals another glance at me. She appears to be thinking about what she wants to say next. Finally breaking the silence, she asks, "Did you miss me after we broke up?"

"Every damn day." My response is just as blunt as her question. I let her know, "Not one day went by that I haven't thought about you. I think of you, even more, knowing you're back in Prattville, so thanks for going out on this date with me."

She opens her mouth, then snaps it shut. She wants to say more, and I want to hear what is on her mind. Correction, I *need* to hear what's on her mind.

"Tell me what you're thinking. Don't shut me out."

"We'll get a chance to talk more over dinner. There's no

need in crashing the date before it begins," she warns with a piercing glare into my eyes.

I train my eyes back on the road and agree, "Fair enough."

When I pull up to the restaurant, I rush around to help Rania out of the car. Gentlemanly, I place a hand on the small of her back and walk her into the busy restaurant. I am happy when she doesn't protest me helping her inside.

A smiling hostess greets us at the door and walks us to our seats. I have reserved a quiet area near the back of the restaurant, where we can have some time to catch up without too many disturbances.

Once seated and our drinks ordered, I admire how beautiful Rania looks under the dim lighting. Gosh, she is so lovely.

"I'm glad you gave me the chance to take you out tonight," I say honestly.

"If I hadn't, you would have never left me alone about it."

"At least you know me well."

She shoots me a stern, teacher-glaring-at-an- unruly-student glare. "After tonight, I will have given you the date you want, so you can't keep pressuring me into more dates," she admonishes.

Oh, trust me, sweetheart. It won't be pressure.

"What if you want to go out with me more after tonight? Of your own will, not because I want you to," I ask.

Her reply is a light chuckle accompanying, "Don't get ahead of yourself, Owen. First, we have to get through tonight."

"That's fair, but you know I've always been an

overachiever," I wisecrack.

When she rolls her eyes playfully and laughs, I feel good about the night being off to a good start. At least, she's not shooting daggers at me with her eyes.

Thirty minutes later, our food has been ordered and served. I'm enjoying a T-bone steak, and Rania picks over a Caesar salad.

I point my fork at her plate. "Is there something wrong with your food? I can order you something else if you don't want a salad," I tell her, then slide my plate her way. "Or you can just have my steak, and I'll eat your salad."

She drops her fork on her plate with a clinking sound and pushes my plate back to me. Meeting my gaze, she says, "No, the food is fine."

"Then, what's bothering you?"

I still myself for whatever she is about to say. I can tell from the look on her face that it's about to be a doozy.

Her brown eyes burrow into my green ones. "Why did you cheat?" she asks as more of an accusation than a question. "You said you would never make me regret the trust I had in you, so why did you do it?"

Now, it was my turn to drop my fork and sit back in my chair. I look at her as sincerely as I can. Staring into the windows of her soul, I think of what I can say to make her believe me this time when I tell her the truth.

"I never cheated on you. I tried to tell you that back in college, but you wouldn't talk to me. I know what you saw in the pictures, and I know what Jasmine told you, but it never happened the way they say it did."

"And just how did it happen, Owen!" she grates out through pursed lips.

I continue to explain my side of the story. "Chantel and Jasmine planned it out. Jasmine had her camera ready for Chantel to take advantage of my slow reflex due to the alcohol we were drinking at the party. When Chantel kissed me, I pushed her off of me, but Jasmine had already caught on camera that split second where Chantel's lips met mine. This is something they planned to break us up, and it worked."

"I wish I could believe that, but you looked so into her in that picture that it's hard to believe that you didn't want to kiss Chantel."

"I wish you would believe me, too. We never had a problem believing each other before this happened," I remind her.

"That's because we never had an issue like this. You always made me feel like you wouldn't share something as intimate as a kiss with another woman, but you did. Pictures don't lie, Owen. You had your eyes closed and everything." Her voice cracked when she adds, "Like that kiss with her was the best you ever had."

"Let's get one thing straight. You are the best I ever had."

"Then explain why you kissed her like that?"

"I was laying back on the couch resting my eyes. The next thing I knew, she was on top of me, kissing me."

"On top of you, kissing you," she mimics my excuse.

"That's what happened, Rania, so apparently pictures can distort the truth because I didn't want Chantel to kiss me," I retort.

Rania glances down at the table. "Uh-huh."

"What does your heart tell you happened, Rania? Does your heart call me a liar, or does it tell you to believe me?" I ask.

Her gaze meets and locks onto mine. "When I look into your eyes as you explain to me what happened, my heart tells me to believe you."

I open my mouth to tell her to trust her heart.

She cuts me off. "But hearts lie. That's why we have to use our minds."

I reach my hands out across the table with my palms up. For a moment, I think she's going to resist, but then, she places each of her tense hands into mine.

"Rania, listen to your heart. But more than anything, listen to logic. I waited for you while we were in college. You were a virgin, and I waited because I loved you, still love you. I wanted nothing more than to share your first time with you. Our first time together was magical. Girl, I was ready to propose to you that night. I didn't want anyone else. I couldn't even get hard for anyone else. Before we made love, I pleasured myself many nights and was teased and joked on by my frat brothers because I wasn't getting any. I didn't give a fuck because I knew what I wanted. Then, this thing with Chantel happens at the party, and Jasmine takes pictures of it, and I'm on the outs with you. That had me so bummed. I haven't been able to find anyone who lived up to you since you left me. Not one woman. That's because we're supposed to be together. You're the one for me."

Rania's hands relax in mine. Her alluring eyes melt my gaze and turn me further into mush. Her voice softens when she speaks again. "Let's just say I believe you. Why didn't you find me in all of this time?"

"I tried. You left the University of Alabama and a cool trail behind you. You didn't want to be found."

She laughs. "You're right. I didn't want to be found, especially by you."

"See, you made it hard for me. I stayed in touch with your Aunt Mildred. I asked her about you all the time. She wouldn't tell me how to find you, but she gave me updates on how you were doing, where you worked, and if you were happy. She told me that you were happy where you were. It hurt like hell to be apart from you, but your happiness is all that matters to me."

"Life is okay," she admits with a shoulder shrug. "But I'm starting to feel like being back at home isn't all so bad either. I miss it... and some of the people in it." Her eyes sparkle, and once again, she's looking at me like she did before we fell apart. She's looking at me like she loves me. She's looking at me like she's willing to start putting us back together again.

I don't want to read too much into this look. I only want her to never stop looking at me like this ever again. This is the most satisfying date I have had in a while. I knew it would be because I'm with my sweetheart.

Rania slides her hands out of mine. She picks up her fork and gathers a bunch of lettuce onto it before taking a bite. I watch her eat, wishing I could be devoured as erotically as the greens on her plate. I start thinking of ways to get her to come back to the ranch with me after we leave here. It's a long shot, but I believe in miracles.

I pull my plate back in front of me and pick up my steak-filled fork.

The prospect of that miracle deflates when a slender figure approaches our table and comes into view. It's Melissa, a woman I've been dodging like a winter cold. She reaches the table and stops abruptly.

Melissa gives me a pensive stare, then evil glares at Rania like she's about to lose her mind. Scratch that; she's already lost her mind, and that's the reason I never return any of her calls.

"Well, well, well... look who we have here. Owen Clemonte!" Melissa yells like a madwoman and begins a tirade that I know will set all the progress I made tonight with Rania back to the starting line.

CHAPTER

seven

RANIA

Maybe I can believe that Owen didn't sleep with Chantel. I decide for the moment to push it aside and try to enjoy the night. After all, we're no longer in college, and this is the very first time I have put on a sexy dress and felt comfortable on a date with a man since then.

Just as I'm talking myself into trusting Owen, it's as if God himself sends a sign. A slender white woman approaches our table and glares at me as if I've stolen something from her.

Along with the woman's rude interruption is Owen's immediate discomfort.

"Well, well, well... look who we have here. Owen Clemonte!" the woman yells insanely loud.

Owen looks from the woman to me then back to the woman. Suddenly, a man who was pouring his heart out minutes ago has lost his very capable tongue.

"What's wrong, Owen? The cat got your tongue," the ill-tempered woman addresses him snarkily.

Owen points to our food sprawled out on the table to clue the woman in on our private dinner. "As you can see, we're having dinner here, and you're interrupting us," he states the obvious.

"I can see what you're doing, and I don't care about your dinner. Why haven't you called me, Owen?" the woman snipes back.

Owen shovels the juicy piece of steak that was on his fork before the woman walked up into his mouth. "I don't have a reason to call you, Melissa," he says with a mouthful.

Melissa slams a fist down on the table right beside Owen's plate. "Yes, you do have a reason to call me, dammit!"

Owen looks up at his deranged friend. "Melissa, you need to stop it. You're causing a scene." He glances around the restaurant. Then, his worried eyes collide with mine.

"I don't care if I cause a scene. I told you that you should leave me alone if you didn't want anything serious. I told you that I could never be one of the girls you use for your pleasure and throw away when you're done. I told you that you didn't want to see this side of me," Melissa screams.

Owen grates out through clenched teeth, "And that's why I left you alone."

"No, you didn't. You used me. Stop lying in front of her." The woman hits her fist on the table then points at me. "You don't have to do that for the precious black girl that you're always thinking about."

I clear my throat and reach for my purse. "I think that's my cue to go to the car. I'll let you two talk this out. Owen, the keys," I say and reach my hand out for the keys to Owen's Jeep.

Melissa holds up a hand to halt me. "No, don't leave Raynesha. Not before I tell you how Owen fucks anything with two legs and a pussy. Then, he throws us away because we're not you."

Owen stands and tries to step around Melissa to get to me.

"Do you hear me, Ray—" Melissa's yells are cut off by the restaurant manager.

"Ma'am, I'm going to have to ask you to leave. We can't have you in here hollering like this. We have other customers who are trying to enjoy their meals," the manager admonishes.

While Melissa is preoccupied with the restaurant staff, Owen walks around her. I start walking toward the door. He reaches out to touch my back to guide me to the car. I shrug him off of me and speed up. I don't want to feel his touch right now, not after Melissa's display.

The mood of the night has gone from tentatively giving him another chance right back to 'fuck you, Owen!' I accept him opening the door for me because I don't have another choice. He has the key, and he beat me to the handle.

I don't care who opens the door. All I can think about is getting home and away from Owen and the disgruntled woman he's been avoiding.

I ride silently in the car, arms crossed over my chest until he passes the road to my aunt's house five minutes later. "Where are you going?" I question him.

"To the ranch. We have to talk."

"No, no, no. You should talk to Melissa because you two seem to have some things you need to work out. Not us," I tell him.

"We—as in you and me—are the only two that matter. And we're going to the ranch to talk," he says as a command.

"Fine. Hopefully, after we talk tonight, you'll understand how over we are."

Owen doesn't respond to that. He drives quietly through the dark, desolate roads leading to his family's ranch. When we pull up into his driveway, nostalgia hits me at once. This place used to be a place of refuge once I got my driver's license.

I would run away from high school stress and the busy world and come out here just to be at peace with the land and nature. The smell of pure earth. A horse's neigh in the distance. The barn house sitting miles back from the road. Just like in high school and university, it all relaxes me.

"Back in the day, your father would have been standing on the porch with a shotgun in his hand by now." I can't help but revisit memories of Mr. Hank.

"Yeah, he always thought that he would have to defend the barn from some type of takeover." Owen chuckled with remembrance dancing through his eyes. "You remember that?" he asks.

"Of course, I remember everything about you and your family."

His smile slips. "Come on inside."

Owen walks into the small barn-style house and disappears into the kitchen with, "I'll be right back."

While alone, I admire the brown stucco and dark furnishings that still give off the warm feelings they did years ago. Everything is in its same place except for a suitcase by the doorway. I can't help but admit to myself that this place still feels like home.

Owen walks back into the room with a mug in his hand, and I do everything I can to not smile when I realize what's inside the cup.

"Here, I fixed it just the way you like it," he says and sets the mug down on the table in front of me.

The scent of cocoa, peppermint, and warm milk waft through the air and make me lose the battle of containing my smile. I kick my shoes off and sit on the couch, legs folded underneath me.

"Are you going somewhere?" I ask.

He scrunches up his face. "No, why?"

"The briefcase at the door."

"That's Anson's. He just got back from a business trip in Texas."

"Oh." I don't know why, but knowing that Owen is not leaving the city makes me feel at ease. I pick up the cocoa from the table and inhale deeply from the cup.

It's not until I notice Owen staring at me that I realize how comfortable I am here. I readjust myself and put my feet on the floor and slide back into my shoes, not willing to get caught up in the comfort of being at Owen's home.

I set the mug of what I know is delicious cocoa on the coffee table and bring us back to the reason I'm here. "What do you want to talk about?"

"Rania, you don't have to act all formal here. You can take your shoes off and relax," he says, showing his obvious disappointment with the about-face I just took.

Catching myself from getting too familiar with Owen is the only way I know to protect myself from more heartbreak. "Sorry, not sorry, but I have to keep things on the appropriate level. I'm relaxed enough like this," I assure him.

Owen lets out a long breath. "Okay, you asked me earlier if I missed you when we broke up. I told you the truth. I missed you like crazy, Rania. I did. Now, I have a question for you. Did you miss me?" he asks.

"Yes."

He closes his eyes and lets out a long sigh. "You have to know that you're the only woman I truly ever loved. I didn't sleep with Chantel when we were together. When you accused me, at that time, I hadn't even touched her."

"What do you mean at that time? Did you sleep with her before I accused you?"

"No, I swear," Owen says.

Relief washes over me. *Thank God.*

"What I'm saying is that I never had sex with Chantel when we were together."

Why doesn't he just come out and say he never slept with her? The vague phrases he adds to his denial only makes me have more questions.

I tilt my head to the side and brace myself for the answer to the question I'm about to ask. "What about after we broke up, Owen?"

Owen looks away from me and rakes a hand through his wavy thick dark blond hair. He wears a weary expression. "It was only a few times."

"Fuck you, Owen! How long did it take you to sleep with her after I broke up with you?"

"Don't do this, Rania. Leave the past in the past and just know that she never meant anything to me."

"How long, Owen?" Rania spits out.

"A week or so, okay! After we moved out of the dorm, a few of us went to Tampa over a long weekend. It was a long, drunk week for me. Most of the time, I was drunk and angry that you accused me of doing something I didn't do, so I fucked her! Are you satisfied now?"

Slap! The sound of my hand meeting flesh sounds off in the room.

"Shit!" Owen grates out, rubbing his palm against his reddened cheek. "Did that make you feel better? Here." He turns his other cheek. "Have a go at that one if it will make you forgive my stupidity."

As if it's in slow motion, I rear back and contact his other cheek with more force. Owen's green eyes widen with a glimmer of desire. I know like hell he's not turned on by my anger. That enrages me even more.

"Take me home!" I scream.

"Rania, wait..." He makes a bold move and inches closer to me. Owen is within a foot of me when he reaches out to touch my face. "Stay, and let's talk this out, sweetheart."

Strange, enigmatic energy passes between us. I feel myself giving in as he strokes my cheek and looks down into my eyes. I should stay and talk to him. This is all in our past. We could have a future together. Those are the things I tell myself before I snap out of his entrancing gaze. Looking into his mesmerizing green eyes is a trick. It's sorcery. He's a spellcaster. He has always been this way.

I will myself to look away and tell him, "We have already talked. I've heard enough."

Hearing that he didn't sleep with Chantel while we were together but that they jumped into the sack right after we broke up doesn't make me feel any less betrayed. It makes me think he was feeling her the whole time she was fawning over him.

The signs were there, many of them. Back when we were in university, I had often walked into places Owen hung out with his friends and found him sitting close to Chantel, laughing at her jokes, and enjoying her company despite knowing how I felt about her. It all makes sense now.

I walk out of his reach to stand by the door, done talking and done indulging Owen's confessions. "I'm ready to go, so take me home."

"I will take you home, but this conversation isn't over," Owen finally relents and grabs his keys off the counter so that we can leave.

OWEN

I toss and turn in bed before bolting upright. The upper half of my bare chest is drenched in sweat. My eyes automatically glance at the digital clock near my bedside. It's a little past two a.m. in the morning.

"Fuck!" I sift my fingers through my unruly head of hair before flopping back onto the fluffy pillow. I close my eyes and try to force myself back to sleep but to no avail.

I let loose a long breath trying to slow my racing heart and sling a forearm over my eyes as images from my dream emerge through my lust-filled brain. The first time I took Rania plays through my head like a fucking film on replay.

My mind doesn't want to deal with the reality of what happened earlier tonight. I don't want to think about our hearts broken and our relationship ruined. I only want to remember a time when Rania was beside me, beneath me, all around me, giving me everything I ever wanted and needed.

I'm truly fucked.

After a while, I realize there is no going back to sleep. I sit up in bed, flinging back the bedcovers, and swing my legs over the side of the king-sized bed. I stand and let out another exhale as I glance down at my rigid cock covered by a pair of thin blue pajamas. I adjust the budge before I make my way from my bedroom down the stairs to the kitchen.

Running a hand across my eyes, I let a final breath escape. My heart is still hammering against my chest, and my cock is still throbbing from my elusive dream.

I wish I could will my cock to deflate, but no way would it happen with the dream still fresh on my brain. I rub against the vast expanse of my chest, trying to ease me doing something irrational like getting dressed and driving over to Rania's to claim what's mine.

What has always been mine.

Rania made it clear when she demanded I take her home earlier tonight that she doesn't want to talk to me right now, but I feel the urge to do something to change her mind.

"Think. Don't be fucking stupid, Owen," I try to reason with myself.

I inhale and exhale, letting my breaths out in measured increments before muttering, "Calm the hell down."

In bare feet, I stride through the swinging doors of the kitchen. I flick on a light before heading over to the refrigerator. I allow the cold air of the fridge to wash over me when I open it.

My eyes land on the six-pack of beer that beckons to me

at the moment.

I chuckle. "Yeah, like beer will cool me down," I mutter between stiff lips.

I grab a beer and twist off the metal cap before tilting it to my lips and taking a long swig. I lean up against the counter and take another. I wipe the residue from my lips with the back of my hand.

My cock throbs. Its rigidness demands to be satisfied, but I know it won't be getting its wish anytime soon. I roll the chilled bottle across my chest, still attempting to calm the hell down. I take another long pull and drain the contents before walking over to the nearby trash to dispose of the bottle. I pull out a chair at the oval wooden rustic kitchen table and plop down onto the seat.

Memories of my dream no longer held at bay permeate my thoughts. A dream where my big hands pull Rania's succulent thighs apart to get my first taste of her sweetness. She was a virgin when we were at university. I couldn't believe she—this special woman—was allowing me to be her first. I felt like a fucking king for the privilege that I can only hope to have again in this lifetime...

"Are you sure you want this?" I ask, making sure that she is okay every step of the way.

"Yes!" Rania whimpers as my thumb sweeps across the slick opening of her entrance. Her thighs spread wider, and my breath catches in my throat. Her scent enthralls me. I'm like a fish tethered on the end of her hook. Caught hook line and sinker.

Truly and utterly fucked even before I have my first taste.

My teeth lightly scrape against Rania's labia, and she trembles beneath my tutelage.

"You like it?" I ask with my voice vibrating against her sensitive flesh.

"Oh my God. Owen!"

"I'm going to make this so good for you," I promise her.

"I know you will. I trust you. I love you so much, Owen."

My heart swells from Rania's words. I lift my head, and my green eyes meet her heated stare. "I love you more, sweetheart. I promise I will never make you regret the trust you have in me," I vow to her.

My head delves down to her pussy, and I take my first lick. Dear mother of Jesus, Rania is by far the sweetest thing I ever tasted. My tongue delves deeper and swirls around her tight entrance. Rania's moans and sighs spur me on to ravish her like I have craved to do for so long.

"Ahh, Owen, I'm coming," she cries out, tightening her legs against the sides of my head.

I growl into her saturated pussy and lick and sample her decadence until she pushes me away from her overstimulated clit.

I take one more long lick before crawling up her body, trailing soft kisses as I make my way upward. "Can you feel how much I want you?" I ask her as I settle my latex covered erection against her mound.

God only knows how much I want to go bareback into her... But I know Rania only started taking the pill a little over a week ago. I need to keep my promise and protect her in all things as I promised.

I stroke Rania's cheek softly with the back of my hand before cupping her face to stare deeply into her eyes.

"I want this. I want all of it. Make me a woman," Rania whispers softly as my cock moves into position at her slick opening.

"Oh, god. You're killing me. Thank you for giving me this precious gift," I grunt out as I place a hand around my cock. I begin to push inside Rania's slick entrance, rocking slowly towards my destination. The first bit of me inside her warmth feels amazing; Rania stretches around my massive erection to perfection.

Her nails rake against my back. She moans softly as I go deeper. I finally hit her barrier. I grit my teeth to force myself to keep it slow.

"Are you ready, sweetheart? I don't want to hurt you, but—"

"I know," Rania cut me off. "Just do it. I want this," she barely gets out before I push through the thin barrier and lay claim to her very soul.

"Ahhhh," she screams and bites into my shoulder to stifle her cry. Rania's walls clench around my cock, and I exhale on a grunt.

I am finally home.

"I'm sorry." I still my movement while capturing her gaze.

"No, don't be sorry. I wanted this... I needed this just as much as you. Make love to me, Owen."

I bend my head to capture her lips. "See how good you taste," I mutter.

Rania moans as our tongues intermingle, and I feel like I'm exhorted to another universe inside her heat.

"Never give my pussy away. Promise me."

A low whimper escapes her lips, and my cock throbs inside her tightness.

So. Fucking. Tight.

Our lips part and I put my forehead against hers. Our breaths intermingle as I continue to rotate my hips and move inside of her.

"I love you so much, Owen."

"I love you too. Rania, there will never be another woman for me. No one else. Just you." I drive further into her slick core with each word. Her hips lift and meet mine, and I pick up speed as I penetrate. "Do you feel what you do to me? Do you see how fucking undone you make me?"

"You make me feel the same," she whispers and swivels her hips in a sexy circle.

"You're going to make me come."

"Come for me, Owen."

"Come with me again. I need to feel your sweet pussy clench around me when I come inside you."

Rania shakes her head. "I can't come again this soon. I want you—"

"You can, and you will," I grunt out and slide a hand between our slick bodies. I swirl her wet clit with my thumb and forefinger. I give it a light pinch.

"Owen!" Rania's hips jerk off the bed.

I thrust deeper and faster into her heat. I withdraw and push forward again. My breathing becomes erratic as I pound her soft flesh with mine.

Her pebbled nipples against my chest have me bending my head to take one dark brown nipple into my mouth.

"I'm coming," Rania cries out, and her sweet pussy convulses around my cock.

My fingers continue to work against her clit. I seat myself with a final thrust deep inside her quivering walls and grip her hips as I plunge. Harder. Deeper.

I'm fucking coming!" I grunt out between clenched teeth. I lose myself in the orgasmic bliss as passion spreads inside me and my latex covered cock catches the spurts of my cum.

When we get our breathing under control, I flip over to pull Rania close against my chest.

I never wanted to let her go, and I promised that day with her in my arms that I never would. That day was the one and only time that I laid claim to Rania's body before all shit hit the fan.

"Brother, what are you doing up?" The voice of my oldest brother, Anson, pulls me from my thoughts.

"Rania," I admit.

"Oh, right. How was your date? Do you want to talk about it?"

"Yeah. How long do you have?"

"For you, little brother, as long as you need," he replies, giving me a grin.

I take my brother up on his offer. In the early hours of the morning, I talk, and my brother listens to me bare my soul.

CHAPTER *nine*

RANIA

Monday morning, I walk through the café. The town's early birds are out in full force for their usual breakfast meals and coffee. Aunt Mildred is still in rehab, and I'm doing my best not to think about Owen.

I still can't believe he hooked up with Chantel only a week after breaking up with me. There is no way he could have truly loved me if he went on to sleep with her after her and Jasmine's shenanigans broke us up.

I push those thoughts aside and balance the serving tray in my hand as I walk to a corner table in the café.

"Good morning, Mr. Finney. You having your usual today?" I greet the graying gentleman as I set down a cup of coffee in front of him with two creams and four sugars.

He beams up at me with a toothy grin. "Yep, ya know me—grits and bacon, as always."

"Coming right up."

Mr. Finney opens a pack of sugar and pours it into his cup. "Ya know, Mildred outta keep you 'round here, Rania. Ya just as good at this as she is."

I shush him. "Don't say that too loud. Some of her cronies might go back and tell her that I'm stealing the affection of her regulars," I tease.

"Oh, no. Say it loud and clear. She is the best server in here right now. Mildred did good to call her back home," a familiar voice chimes in from behind me.

I turn to see none other than Owen's brother, Anson, standing there looking like a slightly older, taller version of Owen.

"Mr. Finney, your food will be out shortly," I assure him, then turn and walk toward the kitchen. "Hi, Anson," I say in passing.

"Whoa. Is that all the greeting your big brother gets after all this time?" He pushes my shoulder softly. "Look at you! You've grown up to be a lady."

It's no doubt about it; the Clemonte brothers all have the same charming personalities and heartwarming smiles.

"Thanks. You have also grown up to be a man," I tease, pushing his shoulder in retort.

"Once you put Old Man Finney's order in, can I talk to you for a second?" he asks.

"Sure. Give me a second." I continue toward the kitchen, wondering what Anson has to say to me.

Anson is sitting at a table, talking to Sandra when I come back out with Mr. Finney's food.

"Alright, here you go. Grits and bacon and I had them add a few pieces of bacon for you. Do you need anything else?" I ask Mr. Finney.

"Nope, I think ya got it all and then some. Thank ya, young lady," he says, diving into his plate as I walk away.

Anson is alone now, so I head over to his table and stand beside it.

"You wanted to talk to me?" I ask.

"Sit down, please."

"Look, if this is about Owen—"

"Just have a seat, and let's talk for a minute."

Sighing, I slide into the booth. "Okay, I'm sitting. What's up?"

Anson rests in his seat. "Let me tell you a story about a young man who was so hurt when he couldn't find his girl that he sabotaged his own world..."

Anson begins a long story, explaining Owen's thought process and how hurt he was when I ghosted him. He says Owen slept with Chantel in an attempt to numb the pain.

"He talked to me right after he did it, and he was messed up in the head, drunk crying and talking about how much he missed you. He only used her that week they were on vacation to try to get over you. But he never got over you. Even now, there is no girl that he has ever dated who doesn't know about you."

"He tells them about me? Why?" I ask, remembering the disdain in Melissa's voice when she mentioned Owen talking to her about me.

"Yes, he tells every woman he talks to about you. Every one of them knows about Rania, the one that he really loves," Anson explains.

"I had no idea that he still felt this way about me. I thought he didn't care after all this time. And when he told me he slept with Chantel so soon after we broke up, it made me feel like what we shared was meaningless." Admitting this to Anson conjures up old feelings and new ones I didn't know I had for Owen.

"I know I'm his brother, and it's a given that I'm on his side, but I wouldn't lie to you about this. Owen never cheated on you with Chantel while you were together. When you two got together in college, it was his dream come true. He wanted you in high school, but he was the popular boy, and you were the girl that had so much going for her. He didn't know how to tell you then. So, when you two hooked up in college, he was all about you. He didn't want anything to break you two up."

"He still let her hang off of him to the point that it was annoying. He didn't set boundaries with Chantel, and neglecting to do that allowed all of this to happen."

"I know, and he has regretted it every day since his graduation day," Anson states.

Owen didn't cheat, and he hasn't loved anyone since we broke up. I take a moment to let those revelations sink in. I give myself a chance to think that maybe, just maybe, I have been wrong about him.

"I will talk to him again," I decide.

"I think that would be good. I can tell from the look in your eyes that you miss him too. You two need each other."

It takes everything in me not to admit that Anson is right. "I have to get back to work," is what I say instead.

Just as I slide out of the booth, the door chimes. A medium-sized blond woman walks into the café and glances around the room as if she's looking for someone but is not sure they're here. Spotting Anson, she walks over to the table where he is sitting.

Standing beside the table, I hear the woman, who I now clearly see is Chantel, ask, "Where's Owen? I stopped by the ranch and saw a Jeep with OWEN on the tag, but no one came to the door. He's dodging me."

Anson smirks. "Maybe he doesn't want to talk to you."

Chantel laughs Anson's remark off. "Boy, you must be blind. Look at me. Of course, he wants to see me." She takes a spin, showing off her toned legs, thick hips, and flat stomach. "Besides, I drove all the way down here to visit some old friends and want to see him before I head back home." Chantel winks at Anson. "I'm sure he wants the same."

"I wouldn't say that," Anson says in a tongue-in-cheek manner.

"Talk to you later, Anson," I speak up and get ready to excuse myself.

Chantel glances at me, studying me as if I am an exam she's trying to pass. "Rania?"

"Yeah?"

"Oh, my gosh. I didn't know that was you!" Her feigned

excitement is so blatantly clear to anyone with eyes. " When did you come back to Prattville?" she asks.

"Why do you care about when I come to my hometown?" I spit out, unwilling to pretend that I'm happy to see her. "A better question is, what are you doing here?"

She smirks. "Oh, I came to see Owen. Isn't that obvious?"

"Setting your same old thirst traps, I see," I mumble while checking out her skimpy outfit. "Good luck with getting with Owen again. You're going to need it," I quip.

Chantel chides, "Girl, you wish!"

I chuckle heartily. "Seems like the only girl still starved for attention after all these years is you, and if you ask me, it's pretty pathetic!"

"No one asked you," Chantel shoots back.

Seeing that this back and forth will lead nowhere fast, Anson stands and takes Chantel by the hand. "Let's go, Chantel," he barks and guides the woman who's still sniffing around for Owen out of the café.

I hope this is the last time I see her.

CHAPTER
ten

OWEN

A little after noon, Anson walks into the house and comes into the living room, where Lance and I are watching a football game. Anson takes a seat on the sofa beside Lance and gives me a serious look.

"Chantel is a problem, man," he says.

"What are you saying, bro?" I ask.

Anson lets out a sigh. "I just left Mildred's Café. I went there to get some breakfast."

"Okay. What happened at Mildred's?"

"I talked to Rania, and I think I convinced her of how messed up you were about your breakup," Anson reveals.

"That's good. I'll take all the help I can get in helping Rania see how much I love and miss her. But why does it feel like there is something else you're not telling me? And what is it about Chantel that makes you think she's still a problem?" I ask, my anxiety level rising with each passing second.

"Because she is," Anson insists.

"Well, stop being cryptic and spit it out, bro," I urge him.

Anson leaned forward in his seat. "When Rania and I were done talking, Chantel came into the restaurant and walked right over to my table."

I feel a major headache come on as soon as I hear that Chantel is in Prattville and has stopped by Mildred's Café. "What is she doing in Prattville?"

"She says she's here visiting friends, and she's trying to get in touch with you. Her exact words were, 'Where's Owen? He's dodging me.' And—"

"Rania heard her," I finish his statement.

Anson nods. "Yep. She was standing up to go into the kitchen when Chantel approached the table."

"Shit! I'm fucked!"

"More like bullshit," Lance speaks up. "We all know Chantel is not here visiting friends. I'd be willing to bet she saw those pictures Rania posted on social media—the ones where she was at the café, mentioning that she was in Prattville helping her aunt for a while. Seeing those pictures made Chantel drive down here just to get under Rania's skin," Anson surmises. "Some people can be petty like that."

I can feel the blood coursing through my veins. "I bet you're right. I found out too late that Chantel has always had it out for Rania. She's just here to stir up trouble."

"And after the display today, you gotta go big or go home with Rania. It's going to take a lot to get her back now," Anson advises me.

"Was it that bad, bro?" I ask.

"Put it like this, they didn't stab each other only because there were no knives nearby," Anson recalls.

"Fuck! I don't know why Chantel would come to town, acting as if we still have something going on because we don't."

Lance looks down at his phone. "Shit, man, I have to take this call, but you should put your ass in gear and go get your woman, like right now. Don't give her more time to sit around stewing about the way Chantel rolled up in Mildred's Café to show off in front of Rania."

I let out a slow breath. "I hear you, brother."

"I wholeheartedly agree with Lance. You can't let this ride for long," Anson adds as he stands to his feet. "I'm about to grab a quick shower. I have a meeting in about an hour," he announces.

"Okay, and Anson?"

"Yeah?"

"Thanks for talking to Rania for me."

"Anytime, bro."

Anson walks off to his corner of the house, leaving me to think about how Chantel showing up made Rania feel. I have to figure out a way to let Rania know that she's the one for me—the only one.

Aunt Mildred has already thrown her hat in to help me get Rania back. Besides hunting Chantel down and giving her a piece of my mind, how else can I convince Rania that we were meant to be together?

"I got it!" A devilish grin spreads across my face. A plan is forming in my mind. I pick up the phone and make a few calls until I get the phone number of the one person I think can come to town and make a difference.

"Hello, Janae, this is Owen."

"Hello, Owen. Is everything okay? My mother told me that you called her and asked for my number."

"Yes, I did. Sorry to bother you like this, but this is important."

"What's going on?" Janae sounds concerned, rightfully so since I have never called her before.

"As you know, Rania is back in town," I begin.

"Yeah, she called me and told me she was coming back to help her aunt. Is everything okay with Mildred?" Janae asks.

"Yes, she's healing and will be back to work in a few weeks." I make a mental note to call Mildred to check on her when I end this call.

"Good. Then, what's the problem?" Janae asks.

"Me and Rania. We're the problem."

I explain everything from the day that the misunderstanding with Chantel's picture happened to Chantel reemerging and showing up at Mildred's Café. I even tell her about Melissa and the women I've been with since Rania.

It's been years since I have been with Rania. I don't owe anyone an explanation for my life, but I feel compelled to tell it all to Janae. I want her to know that there have been no true ties to any other woman since Rania.

"If you love Rania so much, why sleep with Chantel, the girl that broke yawl up?"

"At the time, I would have done anything to get Rania out of my system. I couldn't have her, and it hurt like hell. I was so bummed the night I had sex with Chantel. I was just doing something to feel anything other than the hurt. The entire time I was with her, I thought of Rania," pours out of me. "But as I said, I never cheated when we were together. I didn't mess up until she left me."

"I guess in a twisted way, it sounds like you really love her."

"I do—a lot. More than you will ever know. Can I let you in on something that I have never shared with anyone else before now?" I ask.

"I don't know. Should I brace myself for madness?" she half-joked.

"No, just listen to this. It's a song I wrote for Rania."

Janae gasps, showing her shock. "You wrote a song for our girl, Owen? Aw, how sweet."

I begin to sing the lyrics of *Sometimes Rania*.

> *Sometimes Rania,*
> *I lie awake thinking*
> *No, not thinking...*
> *Wondering if I affect you*
> *The way you affect me*
>
> *Sometimes Rania,*

I wonder if you miss me
The way I miss you
If I cross your mind
The way you cross my heart

Sometimes Rania,
I think of you
Grasping for a fiber of you
As I cross life's dangerous highways
Always thinking of you
Like a long walk in the countryside
Like the country girl that's mine

Sometimes Rania,
All I can think about is you.
Sometimes,
I wish I never hurt you.
Sometimes Rania,
I want to erase the past
Sometimes,
I want to make it last

Sometimes every day,
I want to fall in love
All over again.
With our hearts all in.
Like only we can do

When we're in love...me and you.

I sit in my lounger chair in disbelief that I just shared my song with anyone. It had only been my personal therapy whenever I longed to be with Rania.

"Whenever I couldn't be near her, I wrote songs, poems, even a few short stories. I couldn't be with her, so I would just pick up my pen and write a love scene for me and Rania. It was my private way of dealing with my feelings for her. I did this for a long time, not sleeping with anyone else for over a year after my mistakes with Chantel."

"It's time to get you two back together. I was just going to talk to her about it, but after hearing your song, I think we have to be more extreme at this point. You two *have* to get back together," Janae says through teary excitement.

"I want that so much. What do you have in mind? I'm down for whatever you think I should do," I acknowledge.

"Just leave the planning to me. I'll come up with something. Let me check my calendar. Oh, my gosh, this just seems so right. Valentine's Day is in a week."

"I know. Everything happened in perfect time. Mildred needing Rania to come home to help her just in time for Valentine's Day..."

I pause and think about Mildred's ultimate plan. She had planned her surgery so that Rania would have to be here during Valentine's holiday. That thought makes me smile.

"It's too perfect not to give it a shot! I'll text you the details soon," Janae assures me. "Stay by your phone."

"I will, and thanks, Janae."

"You're welcome, and if it means anything, I always

knew you loved her. I also knew you would fall for Chantel's BS if you had a weak moment. That's why I tried to keep you and Rania informed about the games happening around you."

"I wish I could have seen the games Chantel was playing, but I didn't think I had to do more because I let everyone know I loved Rania and didn't care about their feelings about it."

"Well, Owen, I hope you two can put this behind you soon. For what it's worth, I'm on your side now. Look for a call or text from me by tomorrow."

"I sure will." I hang up the phone feeling hopeful. I love and miss my girl, and now that she's back in the same city as me, I want her back in my arms.

Later that day, I take the ride to the rehab facility to see Mildred. She's sitting up in a red leather side chair and dressed in a red sweater with Be Mine written across the front of it.

"Oh hey, Owen. I wasn't expecting to see you here," she beams.

"Hey, Mildred. You know I had to come to see my friend. I've been missing you at the diner," I tell her.

"Well, I brought in the best substitution for me that

there is. Have you made up with my niece yet?" she asks.

"You waste no time in asking the tough questions, I see." I sink down into the chair on the opposite side of the room and sigh.

"Well, are you even close to making up with her?"

"No, but I have a good feeling things are about to change soon."

She smiles. "I hope so. It's a dang-on shame to see the girl wandering around New York pretending to be a city girl. She knows good and well she should be in Prattville, living on your ranch and making me some grand-nieces," Mildred fusses.

I laugh at her canny remarks. "I agree that she should be with me, but I think Rania can make it anywhere. She can thrive in a small town like Prattville, Alabama or in the middle of New York, New York. Our girl is brave and smart," I brag with pride.

An abundance of love is in the huge smile that spreads across Mildred's face. "See, that's why I've been trying to get you two together. You don't play 'bout my niece. I love the way you defend her honor."

I reply, "You planned this, didn't you?"

"Planned what?" Rania comes into the room. Her pink dress bringing in the rays of the sun along with her glowing brown skin.

Mildred thinks fast and quips, "He's talking about this Be Mine shirt I planned to wear for Valentine's Day."

I smile, knowing for sure now that Mildred planned her surgery during Valentine's holiday so that I could make

Rania mine again.

I stand and gesture for Rania to take my chair. "Here, have a seat…"

She declines the offer with a shake of her head. "Go ahead and sit back down. I'll stand."

I walk over to stand by her, leaving the chair open in case she decides to sit down later. "How are you, Rania?"

She stares up at me with an unreadable expression. "I'm doing good. How about you, Owen?"

"I'm fine, sweetheart. Can we talk for a moment? In the hallway?" I ask, happy that she doesn't glare at me for calling her sweetheart.

Aunt Mildred doesn't give her a chance to respond. "Go on and talk to him, Rania. I'll be here when you get back," she injects.

Rania nods. "Sure, let's talk."

"You look beautiful," I tell her once we're alone in the hallway.

"Thanks. You don't look bad yourself. Now, what is it that you want to talk about?"

"I need to apologize for what happened during our date, for Melissa interrupting us and our argument at the ranch. I wanted things to go a lot differently," I tell her.

"It's behind us now. No need in talking about it anymore," she responds.

She's standing at least four feet away, allowing enough room for a cool breeze to move between us. I fight the urge to haul her closer to me and put an end to the chilling distance.

"Does that mean we can move forward from the past? I mean, move forward together," I clarify.

"I had a talk with Anson and took some time to think about everything," she says.

"He told me that Chantel came to the café. Sorry about that. I will talk to her." Just the mention of Chantel's name again makes Rania tense and me angry.

"No, I don't want you to talk to her. I want you to keep ignoring her the same way you have been. When she realizes that there is nothing here for her, she will slither back to the hole she came from," Rania says.

"You're right. She will."

Rania takes a step toward me but only one. "Listen, Owen, we both were young and impressionable back in university. You hung out with your frat buddies a lot, and I was with Janae when I wasn't studying or with you," she recalls.

"Yes, we had outside influences on our relationship."

Rania nods. "When I saw the picture of you and Chantel, a girl I caught hanging off of you too many times, I couldn't see anything but what the picture was telling me. I didn't stop and think about how you always made it known who you cared about. How you always invited me to be with you, and I didn't come because I was studying. It wasn't until I talked to your brother that I realized my part in this."

"Sweetheart, it's not your fault. I will never blame you for studying instead of hanging out with me; it's the reason you're doing so well now," I tell her, taking a step forward.

She raises a hand to stop me from advancing toward her.

"I know, but I should have trusted you, Owen."

My heart steels. Though I understood why she didn't, I never knew how much I needed to hear Rania admit that she should have trusted me.

"That picture would have made anyone upset. The way you responded to it wasn't the problem. It was the conniving person who set it up to be taken in the first place. They are the ones who intended to do harm. But me," I place a hand over my heart. "I would never hurt you. Not intentionally."

"I believe you," she says.

"And Chantel showing up looking for me today. I have nothing to do with that. I haven't talked to her in years," I explain. "I want no dishonesty or misunderstandings between us going forward."

"At first, I was done all over again when she showed up. Then, I thought about it. She doesn't get to prance into town and make me hate you again. Knowing that she never stole your heart away from me how I thought she did changes everything for me. This time around, I will trust you," Rania divulges the very thing I have yearned to hear from her.

She trusts me. This is music to my ears. She believes me. My girl just dried up all my unshed tears. She trusts me!

I have a strong desire to haul her into my arms and kiss her for all the years we missed. As if she senses my urge to kiss her, she begins to back away from me, creating even more distance than we had before.

"Rania—" I call after her.

"Not so fast, Owen. Maybe we can go on another date one day soon," she says, continuing to walk backward toward her aunt's room.

"I would love to take you out again," I say.

She smiles. "Set it up and let me know."

I smile back. "Okay, tell Aunt Mildred I'll see her soon."

She nods. "Later, Owen."

"Not that much later, sweetheart."

I stand frozen to my spot, watching her curvy silhouette until she disappears into the room. This time, leaving her feels different than any time before.

It feels like something new, something great, is on the horizon. Like the ending of my song, *Sometimes Rania* is about to come true. Like there is a chance that we can fall in love all over again.

RANIA

It's Friday before Valentine's Day, and I still haven't heard from Owen about the date he wanted to go on. I try not to let my mind go where it wants to go. I refuse to think about who he will be spending the holiday with since he hasn't called me.

Thankfully, Janae called early this morning to set up a surprise girl's day out in Montgomery tonight. I happily accepted her offer and prepared for some lakeside entertainment and good food downtown on the riverboat ride.

"When you get home from the café, a package should be in front of the door waiting for you," Janae had said at the end of our call this morning.

"What? What did you get me?"

"Just open it and put it on. No questions asked."

This sounded super suspicious, so I asked, "What are

you up to, Janae?"

"Just put it on..."

We ended our call, and I went on about my morning.

After a long day at the café, I make it home to find a box containing a red bodycon dress with a plunging neckline. I can deal with the fact that it's a figure-hugging dress that dips below the line of my cleavage. Though, the thing that stands out is the barely-there fabric that's damn near nonexistent to cover my thighs.

"Whoa, Nelly!" I immediately call Janae back and protest. "I can't wear this. You know I don't dress like this."

"Yep, and that's why you're wearing it tonight. Put the dress on, and I'll be there at five sharp," is Janae's reply before her name disappears from my phone screen.

I sit there in disbelief. She really hung up. Janae bought me this skimpy dress and then hung up on me.

I mull over the idea of putting on the dress and going out versus finding something else to wear. The temperature is forty-nine degrees in Montgomery today. If I do wear the dress, a huge overcoat will be necessary. My legs feel cold at the thought of being bare in the forty-nine-degree weather. Though I have gotten used to colder temperatures in New York, I still have not completely adapted to the cold weather.

I talk myself out of being a prude and decide to wear the dress with a long overcoat and a pair of leggings in my purse if I need them.

I'm sitting on the Harriett III in Montgomery four hours later, wearing a dress with barely enough fabric to cover my thighs. Six-inch stiletto heels match the dress to perfection. I do look damn good. I just would feel more comfortable if the dress had twice the fabric. I pull at the material once again and look at Janae, who's snapping her fingers to the light jazz playing.

"That's my shit right there. Me and Jonah can make some more babies to this." She stands up and starts swaying side to side to John Coltrane's "In a Sentimental Mood."

The boat is scheduled to take off in a few minutes. Our dinner will be out shortly after that.

I don't know why, but I think about Owen. Even if he doesn't plan a date for us this weekend, I'll be good for the Valentine's Day weekend after spending some time with my old friend. I submit to the idea that I'll only get a Galentine date for this Valentine's holiday.

The servers come around and place our salads and seafood meals in front of us. It looks delicious. "Not bad for a pre-Valentine's Day dinner," I say to Janae.

"It's wonderful. And when we get back, we can stop to listen to Frankie Beverly and Maze. The band is playing live at the lakeside tonight," Janae announces.

She is just full of surprises today.

"Sweet!" I say and begin to pine over the seafood salad in front of me. "This salad looks great. Why didn't you get one?"

Janae peers around me and looks toward the door. "Oh, I didn't want one."

"You're missing out," I tell her.

She looks toward the door again, this time with

squinted eyes.

I turn around and look in the direction that she's looking. "Are you expecting someone?" I ask.

"Who? What? No. Give me a minute. I have to run to the bathroom," she says, then stands up and makes her way toward the exit.

I glance over my shoulder and watch as she hurries out of the room. I shrug and turn my attention back to my salad and start enjoying it.

A few minutes after Janae leaves, the captain announces the boat is about to start its tour. A tantalizing scent wafts by me that makes me look up into the green eyes I have been thinking about all day. The music switches up to Gregory Porter's "Insanity," and lyrics that match the mood make this moment unreal.

> *How did we ever lose our minds?*
> *And fall apart, knowing we're the only ones*
> *To heal each other's hearts*
> *Bring your love back to me*
> *Stop this insanity*
> *Before we go too far*

"Owen, hey," I speak over the music.

"Hey, sweetheart."

Realizing he could be here on a date himself erases the elation I have from seeing him. "What are you doing here?" I ask after the shock wears off.

"I'm here to spend the rest of the night with you."

"Spend the rest of the night with me," I parrot. "Wait, where's Janae?" I look around for her, expecting her to walk back into the room at any moment.

"She's gone to the hotel. She and her husband have a suite there for the weekend."

I've been had, and Janae was a coconspirator in getting me here with Owen. I guess neither of them knows I would have come had he just asked me out.

"You didn't have to do this. When you said you would set something up, I never thought this would be it. You could have just set up a date."

Owen takes the seat across from me. "I wanted to surprise you. I wanted to see this look on your face. I want you to know what it will be like being with me if you give me another chance. I will spend the rest of my life doing whatever it takes to make sure you are always surprisingly happy and never bored," he says with a heart-warming smile.

I scan the direction Janae disappeared to, and she really is nowhere in sight. "You and Janae are going to get it."

Owen adjusts himself in his seat and gets comfortable. "Trust me, sweetheart, I'm looking forward to getting it from you."

Every fiber of my being responds to this statement. My body is fully alive when a song I've never heard before begins to fill the room and my heart.

The DJ announces, "This song is from Owen Clemonte to his sweetheart, Rania Brown."

"It's a song I wrote," Owen confesses as a melody comes over the river boat's speakers.

Owen is singing a song entitled *Sometimes Rania*. There is no real production, just Owen singing on top of a beat. The lyrics explain how he felt when we broke up.

Owen stands and reaches out a hand, "Dance with me."

I accept his hand and follow him to the dance floor, where he hauls me into his arms and sings the lyrics of the song close to my ear. He holds me tight, intimate, and flush to his body. Like he has no intention of ever letting me go.

The words from the song pour into me, and I can't think of anything but Owen. My body instantly comes alive and remembers the feel of his touch. His woodsy, citrusy scent impales my senses, rendering me his once again.

I know it's not a spell this time. It's not a trick. This is the love that was meant to be. The love that was always meant to be.

"You feel so good in my arms, Rania. I just can't stop touching you," he breathes against my ear.

Owen's hands leave no part of my body untouched. The way he palms the globes of my butt cheeks into his hands makes me wonder if the dress is still covering it. I'm so deep into his orbit that I cannot even think enough about it to care.

As if this night is already more than I could have imagined it would be, after the Harriett III pulls back up to the dock, Owen and I sit in the grass and listen to the live concert. Hands intertwined, we listen to each ballad, singing along together wherever we could. And yes, I slipped on my leggings before getting off the boat.

Once we finish singing loudly to Frankie Beverly's "Before I Let Go," Owen makes an announcement. "I have one more thing I want us to do tonight."

He stands and helps me up from my place on the grass. We walk to the edge of the grassy area, and a neighing horse and old-style carriage are waiting for us.

"Owen and Rania?" the driver asks when Owen approaches him.

"Yes, we're ready to go now," Owen replies, then turns and nods for me to get into the carriage.

This is so romantic that I have to internally tell myself to calm down.

We ride around downtown Montgomery, laughing and talking about some of the things we have experienced since those days back at university. Owen brings me up to date on business at the ranch and his personal life. I tell him about some of my accounting clients and dating mishaps.

We know each other. We understand each other.

The carriage pulls back up to the Renaissance, and it feels like we haven't been gone but five minutes. However, when Owen hands the man a hundred dollar bill and says, "That should cover the hour we were gone," I know we have been riding for a much longer time.

My body slides down his as he helps me out of the carriage.

"I really had a good time tonight. Thank you for sharing the night with me. It puts my Valentine's weekend off to a good start," he says.

Though the carriage has pulled away, he still holds onto me, supporting me though I do not need him for support to stand.

"I had a good time too," I rasp out.

An awkward moment of silence hangs in the air as I remember that my ride here is inside the Renaissance Montgomery Hotel getting it on with her husband.

"We should go," Owen says and releases the hold he has on me.

"Yeah, I guess I'll need a ride." I start to walk toward the parking lot.

"Or..."

"We could stay here together," I say what I really want to happen.

Owen wraps an arm around my waist and pulls me into his arms, holding onto me passionately. His lips come crashing down on mine. My tongue works hard to take over the kiss, yet Owen dominates the passion that's igniting both of us.

"Let's get a room," I whisper into his mouth.

"Already have one," he admits.

I draw back and look into his gorgeous green eyes. "So you knew this was going to happen?"

"I didn't know this was going to happen, but I hoped and prayed it would, sweetheart."

I wiggle out of his arms and strike his chest playfully. "Well, your prayers have been answered."

I sashay my tiny dress and legging covered ass, jiggling everything the good Lord gave me in front of him as I walk toward the hotel. Looking back over my shoulder, I watch Owen watch me. "Well, don't meet me there, beat me there," I tease him.

He pries his eyes from my lower half and takes my hand,

pulling me toward the hotel's lobby and his room.

OWEN

As soon as we step into my room, Rania dives into my arms and wraps her legs around me. She's kissing me like she used to—warm, wet, inviting strokes of her tongue that send waves of heat all over my body.

"Oh, baby...You are the most beautiful woman I've ever seen," I blow the words into her mouth as I kiss her.

"Owen..."

She only has to say my name like that once. I know what she wants, what she needs.

My thumbs slide into the sides of her tights. "Are you sure you want this?" I ask, making sure she's okay with us taking this next step tonight.

"Yes!" Rania whimpers, "I want this so bad right now."

She's moving her body in a circular motion on me, grinding on me, reminding me of her rhythm. Merging her aura into mine, she gives me all of her essence to reabsorb as if she thinks I can take it.

I can't take it.

It's been too long since I've been inside of her. I've dreamed of this moment for far too long, and I'm about to lose control.

I walk over to the bed and ease us onto it. Our lips take over the moment my hands caresses her breasts through the plunging neckline of the dress she's wearing as a shirt.

The sound of her sweet moans wrap around me and become part of me. I want to hear her moan again and again tonight.

She starts picking at the buttons on my shirt, removing my shirt within seconds. Next, she's undoing my belt buckle. I never lose contact with her lips as she undresses me.

I strip her clothes away as if I'm a miner, looking for gold and found my treasure.

In record time, we are naked, and my dick is condom clad. Our naked bodies press together as the dance between our tongues continue.

With every breath I take, I breathe her in and assign a different part of her essence to my memory. I want to decode every piece of her, file the memories away, and keep them forever. I want to never forget this moment. Not even forsake the tiniest part of it.

As I deepen the kiss, Rania's hips gyrate, almost undoing me before I can slip inside of her heat.

I leave my position on top of her and kiss my way down to the slick opening of her entrance. I have to taste her at least once before I ride her into ecstasy.

Her thighs spread wider, and my breath catches in my throat. Her scent enthralls me. Her moans drive me insane. Just as in my dreams, I'm like a fish tethered on the end of her hook. Caught hook line and sinker.

Remembrance of her taste dances on my tongue. I am truly and utterly fucked even before I can dive in and get a good taste of her again.

My teeth lightly scrape against Rania's labia, and she trembles. Grabbing at my locks, she moans out her pleasure, "Please, Owen, give it to me. I want to feel you now."

I lift my head, and my green eyes meet her heated stare. "I will, sweetheart. Just let me get a taste."

My head delves down to her pussy, and I take a lick of what I know is the sweetest pussy on earth. My tongue delves deeper and swirls around her tight entrance.

She feels like she did back in university, innocent and untouched as if she's been saving herself for this moment. Just the tiniest chance that this is true spurs me on to ravish her like I have craved to do for so long.

Her hips spring off the bed, and she's fucking my tongue, sending it deeper and deeper inside of her. I hold her in place and assault her clit, intermittently sucking on it and flicking my tongue across it.

"Owen, I'm coming," she cries out, tightening her legs

against the sides of my head. Her hips buck incessantly, and then she goes limp.

I growl into her saturated pussy, licking up her chocolate decadence until I am filled with her sweetness.

I take one more long drink from her before crawling up her body, trailing soft kisses as I make my way upward. I stroke Rania's cheek softly with the back of my hand before cupping her face to stare deeply into her eyes.

"I missed you, Rania," I profess as I settle my latex covered erection against her mound.

"I missed you more, Owen," she says.

"Thank you for giving me this," I grunt out as I place a hand around my cock. I begin to push inside Rania's slick entrance, rocking slowly to enter her.

"Ahhh," she murmurs as she stretches around my massive erection to perfection.

Her tight heat feels amazing. It feels like our first time we made love but damn sure doesn't feel like the last time I'll be inside of her tonight and forever.

Her nails rake against my back, reminding me of the way she tortured me before. Her moans increase as I go deeper into her tightness.

"When was the last time you've been with someone?" I ask.

"I don't know. A few years, maybe," she replies.

A few years. With each ensuing stroke, those three words soak into my psyche and become apart of me. She's been waiting for this moment as much as I have.

I sink as deep into her as her body will allow, and her

walls hold onto my cock for dear life. "Rania, baby..."

"Deeper," she says as if she can sense I've been holding back. "I want all of it," she barely gets out before I push so deep inside of her that it feels like I'll come out the other side.

I am finally back where I belong. This is home.

Rania's walls clench around my cock as if cosigning their agreement. "Ahhhh," she screams and bites into my shoulder to stifle her cry.

I exhale on a grunt, "Never leave me again. Promise me."

A low whimper escapes her lips, and my cock throbs inside her tightness.

Heavens, she is so fucking tight.

"You're going to make me come," I growl out.

Rania is throwing her pussy back to me, giving as good as she is taking. "Come for me, Owen," she commands.

With that said, I fall over the edge of pleasure and take her hard and rough.

Rania moans incessantly, meeting my strokes in earnest. "I'm coming!" she screams out her pleasure into the passion-filled air. "I'm coming, I'm coming, I'm coming!" she moans.

I place a hand between us and begin to apply just enough pressure to her wet clit with my thumb and forefinger to send her freefalling over the edge.

"Owen!" Rania's hips jerk off the bed.

I thrust deeper and faster into her heat. I withdraw and push forward again. My breathing becomes erratic as I pound her soft flesh with my cock and rub her clit with my fingers.

As I pound into her, I put my forehead against hers and demand, "Never leave me, Rania. Promise you will never leave."

Our breaths intermingle as I continue to rotate my hips and move inside of her, imploring her to stay with me and never leave again.

"I'll never leave you," she promises as her body begins to tremble.

"Stay in Prattville. Move in with me on the ranch," I continue my requests.

Her body trembles beneath me. "I'll stay. I'll stay with you," she pants. "Oh, my god. I love you so much, Owen."

"I love you too. Rania, there will never be another woman for me. No one else. Just you." I drove further into her slick core with each word, "You're the only one for me."

"You're the only one for me," she whispers and swivels her hips in a sexy circle. "The only one. Oh, goodness! I'm coming again," Rania cries out, and her sweet pussy convulses around my cock.

My fingers continue to work against her clit. I seat myself with a final thrust deep inside her quivering walls and grip her hips as I plunge hard and deep.

"I'm fucking coming!" I grunt out between clenched teeth.

I lose myself in the orgasmic bliss as passion spreads inside me and the latex catches the spurts of my cum.

When we get our breathing under control, I flip over to pull Rania close against my chest, where I hold her until I roll on top of her and take her again for another of the many times we make love Valentine's weekend.

"Did you mean it when you said you would move back to Prattville?" I question Rania on our ride back to the ranch on Valentine's Day morning.

Her eyes sparkle just like old times when she looks at me. "Yes, I meant it. I'm ready to come back home. I never really was happy in New York. I mean, I love my job and the people I work with; it's just that I was missing something. Missing you."

"I feel the same way. I have been on the ranch, surrounded by all the things I love, nature, farm animals, my brothers, but the one person I want with me was miles away. It will be great having you home."

"Well, I'm coming home finally."

My heart swells with a joy that I can't even express. I lean over and cup her chin, hauling her face to mine. "Welcome back," I say before crashing my lips onto hers.

"I have to call Aunt Mildred and tell her that I'll be staying with her for a while," she says when our kiss ends.

"Nonsense. You can stay with me."

"Now, Owen, you know I can't move right in with you. I think we should take things slowly."

"At no point over this weekend did you ask me to take things slow. You wanted it fast and hard then; we're going to take it fast and hard in our relationship."

"Can we only have hard when in the bed? I don't want hard or complicated," Rania says with a serious expression on her face.

"Baby, I can't promise you times won't get hard, but I will make sure there are no more complications like the ones we have experienced," I tell her.

"Fair enough."

"So, you moving in?" I press.

"Give me two weeks to make the decision."

"Two weeks, and I'm coming to get you and all of your things."

"Okay." She bites down on her bottom lip. "So you really can't live without me, Owen Clemonte?"

"Keep biting down on your lip like that and I'll pull over and show you how bad I can't live without you."

"Let's not get arrested for public indecency today. You know Montgomery police are hiding everywhere," Rania quips.

"They surely are," I say, weaving through Montgomery traffic, headed to the ranch.

We're finally back together where we belong, going to the place we soon will call home. It was a long road to get Rania back into my arms. I know the mistakes I made to lose her, and I will never make those mistakes again.

"Owen, when we were making love, you asked me to promise to never leave you again," she says as if she is reading my mind.

"Yes, sweetheart. You can't leave me like that."

"I won't. I will never leave you without giving you the chance to explain yourself, and when you're explaining yourself, I will give you the benefit of the doubt. Just don't put me in the position where I feel like I have to trust ill feelings that have festered too long."

I cross my heart with my forefinger. "Sweetheart, now that you are mine again, you won't have to worry about any women coming around me. I'll be one of those guys who says, 'if my woman can't come, I can't come.' I'm stuck to you like glue."

She chuckles. "You don't have to be that extreme."

"I disagree. Extreme times call for extreme measures."

"That's why I love you," she says, still laughing at me. "You're funny."

"I won't let either of our hearts get broken again," I profess to her with a deep understanding of the lengths I will go through to make sure these words ring true forever.

"No more heartbreaks," Rania agrees.

We ride to the ranch holding hands, holding onto our forever with every strand of our beings. Maybe we'll build another house on the ranch, just for us. Maybe we'll fill that house with kids.

Whatever we do, we will make it this time. I believe our love, which has not dimmed over the test of time, will last until the end of our days.

KEEP IN TOUCH

SHANI GREENE-DOWDELL:
https://linktr.ee/shaniwrites

THERESA HODGE:
https://linktr.ee/gemini2goddess

ABOUT THE AUTHORS

Theresa Hodge is an Alabama native - loving mother, wife, sister, aunt, and friend. She is at her best when she is able to bring happiness to others. This author loves to read almost as much as she loves to write fictional stories. She finds writing therapeutic at times, especially during the loss of her oldest sister from breast cancer, which birthed her "Ask Me Again" Series. This was her first but this compilation led to her writing several other books. These book's includes her bestselling Noelle's Rock series among many others.
Additionally, Theresa has a love affair with poetry. She began writing poetry at an early age and it served as a catalyst for her growth as a writer.

If Theresa can bring a smile to your face and encourage someone else along her journey, she considers it a blessing beyond measure.

Shani Greene-Dowdell is a writer who enjoys weaving suspenseful romantic stories into page-turners. She has written 30+ novels and assisted countless authors with jumpstarting their writing careers.

Shani writes in the multicultural romance and urban genres. When not reading, writing, or editing, she enjoys exploring nature, taking long walks, and spending time with family. She welcomes all of her readers and supporters as a part of her huge extended family.